5/99

LET ME OFF THIS SPACESHIP!

by **Gery Greer** and **Bob Ruddick**
illustrations by **Blanche L. Sims**

HarperCollins*Publishers*

LET ME OFF THIS SPACESHIP!

Text copyright © 1991 by Gery Greer and Bob Ruddick
Illustrations copyright © 1991 by Blanche L. Sims
For information address
HarperCollins Children's Books,
a division of HarperCollins Publishers,
10 East 53rd Street, New York, NY 10022.
2   3   4   5   6   7   8   9   10

Library of Congress Cataloging-in-Publication Data
Greer, Gery.
   Let me off this spaceship! / by Gery Greer and Bob Ruddick ;
illustrated by Blanche L. Sims.
      p.   cm.
   Summary: When Tod and Billy are kidnapped by creatures from outer
space, they try to make as much trouble as they can on board ship so
that the spaceship captain will take them back to Earth.
   ISBN 0-06-021605-0. — ISBN 0-06-021606-9 (lib. bdg.)
   [1. Extraterrestrial beings—Fiction.   2. Outer space—Fiction.
3. Science fiction.]   I. Ruddick, Bob.   II. Sims, Blanche, ill.
III. Title.
PZ7.G85347Le   1991   90-32045
[Fic]—dc20   CIP
                                                              AC

For Brandon

1

"We're sinking!" said Billy.

"No, we're not," I said. "We're just taking on a little water, that's all."

Billy and I were paddling across Grant Park Pond in the boat we had built that morning. We had named it the S.S. *Jungle Explorer*. It was made out of orange crates and two-by-fours, and it looked really terrific. Sure, it was leaking a bit. But we were not sinking. Billy just tends to worry a lot.

"The *Jungle Explorer*," I said, "will float for a hundred years. We will use it to explore a thousand unknown rivers."

"Tod," said Billy, "my tennis shoes are underwater."

I looked down. So were mine. There was about five inches of water in the bottom of the boat. And more was coming in fast.

Hmmm, I thought. Maybe we *were* sinking.

"This is normal," I told Billy. "Every boat leaks a little on its first voyage. But, uh, I'll tell you what. Maybe we should paddle for shore. Just to be on the safe side."

We paddled for shore. Suddenly, a big new leak sprang open on the left side of the boat. Water gushed in.

"Faster!" I yelled.

We paddled like mad. We leaned forward, giving it our all. Billy's paddle whacked our picnic lunch and knocked it into the water.

"Egg sandwich overboard!" shouted Billy.

"We're better off without it!" I yelled. "We're overloaded. We need to lighten the ship!"

About a gallon of water sloshed over the side and landed in my lap. It was cold. The *Jungle Explorer* was riding lower and lower in the water.

"We're sinking!" I shouted. "Don't be so heavy! You're too heavy! Try to be lighter!"

"I'm trying!" said Billy.

"I just remembered something," I huffed between strokes. "The captain always goes down with the ship."

"Aye, aye, Captain," said Billy.

"Wait a minute," I said. "Who said *I* was the captain?"

3

"You're a natural leader," Billy said over his shoulder. "It's been an honor serving under you, sir."

The boat was filling up fast.

"We're still sinking!" I yelled. "Trim the jib! Report to the quarterdeck! Man the lifeboats!"

Too late.

The front of the boat dipped underwater. A huge wave flooded in, totally swamping us. The boat plunged to the bottom of the pond.

Billy and I both went down with the ship.

Luckily, the pond was only waist deep. We stood up.

Billy looked down into the water with disgust. "The *Jungle Explorer* sank," he said.

I couldn't argue with him. The facts

were on his side.

We waded to shore and collapsed on the grass. We rested in the sun for a while.

After we caught our breaths, we talked about the *Jungle Explorer*.

"Actually," I said, "the *Jungle Explorer* wasn't really such a bad boat. I mean, it was a nice-*looking* boat. It was long and low and streamlined. Of course, it had one or two design problems."

"Yeah, holes," said Billy. "It had holes."

"Right," I said.

Billy glanced at his watch. "Hey, we'd better get going," he said. "We're going to be late."

We were supposed to be at Billy's house by twelve. His mother was making tacos for us, and she wanted us there on time. When Billy's mother says "Be here at noon," she means *"Be here at noon."*

We jumped up and started jogging through the park, taking a shortcut through the woods. We knew this park like the backs of our hands. We had explored every inch of it. We had looked for frogs along Grant Park Creek. We had gone sledding down Grant Park Hill. We had climbed trees in Grant Park Woods. And now, of course, we had sunk our boat in Grant Park Pond.

One thing was for sure, Grant Park was never boring.

"Boats," I said as we jogged along. "You can't count on them. I think we should build a car. Cars can't sink."

"They can crash," said Billy.

"Yeah, but—"

I never finished my sentence.

Because just then we saw it.

A spaceship!

Sitting right there in the middle of the soccer field was a huge silver spaceship!

2

It was *enormous*.

It looked like a giant silver Frisbee standing on short silver legs. With thousands of pale-blue lights all around its edge. It was about the size of our school.

"Wow, neat!" I said. "Somebody spent big bucks on that thing. It must be for a movie."

Billy shook his head. "Movie, nothing," he said. "That thing looks real to me. I think it's from outer space."

I snorted. "Don't be ridiculous. It's

for a movie. It's *supposed* to look real."

"I think we should call the Army," said Billy. "And maybe the Air Force."

Like I said before, Billy tends to worry about things a lot.

"Come on," I said. "Let's take a closer look."

We walked over to the spaceship. It loomed over us like some kind of gigantic spider.

"It looks great, doesn't it?" I said. "It's probably made out of cardboard. Isn't it amazing what they can do with a little cardboard and some silver paint?"

"I think we should call the president," said Billy.

"That's silly," I said. "Here, look. I'll prove it's made out of cardboard."

I went over to one of the spaceship's legs and rapped it with my knuckles.

11

It made a sharp metallic sound.

Billy looked at me. "That didn't sound much like cardboard to me," he said grimly.

"Yeah, uh, well," I said, "they just decided to build the best spaceship money can buy, that's all. It must be a really big-budget movie. It probably has a lot of really famous movie stars in it."

Suddenly, the pale-blue lights began to flash. Thousands of them. In a strange, wild, swirling pattern. Seconds later, a deep, throbbing hum came from inside the spaceship. It sounded like eight or ten giant nuclear-powered engines had just been turned on. The ground shook. The air around us crackled with static electricity, making the hair on my arms stand on end.

"Well, now, Billy," I said quickly.

"This has been fun. But I'll tell you what. See those trees over there? Maybe we should go over and stand behind them for a minute. Just to be on the safe side."

"Now you're talking!" said Billy.

We broke into a gallop. *Nobody* has ever run faster than we did.

We were almost to the trees when the spaceship took off.

With a great rush of air, it shot into the sky and soared toward the clouds.

Billy and I skidded to a stop. We stared up at the sky. *It was a real spaceship!*

Just then we heard someone running. From the trees nearby, a man came bursting out onto the soccer field.

He had two heads!

And silver skin!

And ears shaped like bat wings!

I was pretty sure he had three legs,

13

too, but I was too scared to look.

Both of his heads were looking up into the sky. He was waving his arms wildly. It looked like he was trying to signal the spaceship.

The spaceship paused. It hovered just below the clouds. Then, suddenly— *ZAP! WHOOSH!*—the two-headed man disappeared. I guessed that they had beamed him up into the spaceship.

Billy and I looked at each other.

"How many heads did that man have?" Billy asked me.

"One too many," I said.

"Let's get out of here," said Billy.

"Right!" I said.

But it was too late.

Because suddenly—*ZAP! WHOOSH!*— Billy and I got beamed up, too!

3

Billy and I landed on top of each other on the floor of a large room. The walls glowed with a strange blue light.

I jumped up, pulled Billy to his feet, and shouted, "HEAD FOR THE ESCAPE HATCH! QUICK!"

It was a good plan, but there were a few problems.

First, there was no escape hatch.

Second, I glanced out a porthole and noticed that the Earth was only about the size of a baseball. And it was getting smaller fast.

And third, I noticed that we were

surrounded by about twelve aliens from outer space.

One of them was the two-headed man with three legs. The others were even weirder.

"Forget the hatch," I whispered to Billy. "I guess we'll have to sweet-talk these guys."

"Are you kidding?" whispered Billy. "Take a good look at them."

I did. Most of them looked like the sort of creatures who would swallow a sweet-talker whole.

Still, what else could we do? I stepped forward.

"Greetings, friends," I said. I stretched out my arms in greeting. "I—"

"Seize him!" said one of the two-headed man's heads.

18

"And the other twerp, too!" said his other head.

One of the creatures grabbed me. It looked a little like an octopus standing on long thin legs. Two of its arms shot out and wrapped themselves around my arms like whips. I couldn't move.

Billy was grabbed by a one-eyed kangaroo-type creature. It had scaly green skin and long claws. It tucked Billy under one of its arms.

The two-headed man led the way down a long hallway and into a big round room. A lot of creatures were sitting in front of computers and viewing screens. I figured it had to be the control room.

A tall, thin alien was standing near a star map. He had orange skin and green hair that stuck out in spikes. He looked important.

The two-headed guy hurried over to him.

"We have a problem, Captain," said his first head. "We found these two in the transporter room."

"That's right," said his second head. "We don't know how they sneaked aboard, but they did. Should we throw them in the brig?"

"Who are they?" asked the captain.

"Twerps," said the two-headed guy.

"We're not twerps!" said Billy. "We're Earthlings."

"And we didn't sneak aboard," I said. "We got beamed up by mistake. Billy and I were just standing around minding our own business. And the next thing we knew, here we were."

"A *mistake?*" snorted the two-headed guy. "It was not! You two must have beamed yourselves aboard."

"We did not!" said Billy.

"You did too!" said the two-headed guy.

"Did not!"

"Did too!"

"QUIET!" yelled the captain.

4

Everyone quieted down.

"Release the Earthlings," said the captain.

Billy and I were released.

"Okay, Earthlings," said the captain, "listen carefully. My name is Captain Thorst. Now, I don't know how you got aboard this spaceship. Maybe you beamed yourselves aboard, or maybe we beamed you up by mistake. It doesn't matter. Either way, I'm taking you back to Earth."

"Gee, thanks, Captain," I said. "That's very nice of—"

"I'm taking you back," the captain went on, "just as soon as we complete our scientific missions. We must deliver our sample of Earth's atmosphere to the planet Kanthor."

"Oh?" I said. "We're going to the planet Kanthor first? Would that be in this neighborhood?"

Captain Thorst shook his head.

"Not exactly," he said. "Kanthor is about twenty-six trillion miles from here. You will be gone thirty Earth years."

I gulped. *Thirty Earth years?*

"Sorry, Captain," I said quickly. "We can't make it. We've got baseball practice at four o'clock this afternoon."

"Yeah," said Billy. "And you wouldn't believe all the homework we have for tomorrow."

"So just put us down anywhere," I said. "My house, Billy's house, Disneyland…"

"Impossible," said Captain Thorst. "I have a mission, and I mean to carry it out. Now make yourselves comfortable and stay out of my way for the next thirty years. I'm the captain, and I'm a very busy man."

Actually, he didn't look like a man. He looked more like a giant carrot. But I didn't think it would be wise to point that out.

Captain Thorst turned away and went back to work. All the other creatures went back to work, too.

I pulled Billy over where nobody could hear us.

"We need a plan," I said in a low voice.

A ton or two of purple creature lumbered by. He was mostly teeth.

"You can say that again," said Billy.

We tried to think of a plan. Of course, it was pretty hard to concentrate. All kinds of weird creatures kept walking, waddling, and slithering by.

My biggest problem was a little yellow fellow with long, shaggy hair. He was only a foot high, but he had terrific feet. He probably wore about a size twenty-five shoe. I think I could have liked him okay, except for one thing. He was a kicker. He kept kicking me in the foot.

By the time he got tired and left, Billy and I still didn't have a plan. But we had agreed on a few things. Hand-to-hand combat, surprise attacks, and tackling were out. There was too much monster muscle on their side.

We were going to have to use our wits.

Suddenly, I grabbed Billy's arm.

"I've got it!" I whispered. "What if we make Captain Thorst think that living with Earthlings will drive him crazy? I mean, he's going to have to spend thirty years on this spaceship with us. What if we make ourselves more trouble than we're worth? Maybe he'll turn around and take us back."

Billy's eyes lit up.

"Great idea!" he said. "More trouble than we're worth, huh? That's just what my mother says about me sometimes. This should be a snap."

"Good," I said. "Let's go."

5

I strolled over to the captain, with Billy following behind me.

Captain Thorst was sitting at the control panel. He was busy studying dials and turning knobs. I put my arm around his shoulders.

"Captain," I said, "I think I've got the hang of it."

Captain Thorst stopped and stared at me. "Got the hang of what?"

"The spaceship. I spent a few minutes looking over the control room. And now I think I'm ready to fly this baby."

"What!" sputtered the captain. "You're ready to fly the spaceship? Don't you know that this is a very complicated machine? It takes years of training to—"

"Shhh," said Billy. "Tod is thinking."

I stroked my chin and nodded my head. My eyes moved back and forth across the control panel. There were about a million lights and knobs and buttons and switches.

"Hmmm…" I said. "Planet Kanthor.… Now what's the best way to get there? Straight out past Mars, I guess. And turn right at Jupiter. Yeah, that should do it. No, wait…Hmmm.…"

Captain Thorst turned to Billy. "But," he roared, "we're not going anywhere *near* Jupiter! What's he talking about?"

"Don't worry, Captain," said Billy.

"Tod is very good at directions. You should see him with his bicycle. He knows every shortcut in town."

"That's it!" I cried. "A shortcut! Why should we go all the way over to Jupiter first? We can just cut straight through the middle of the solar system!"

"Huh?" blurted the captain.

"I'm glad you agree," I said. "RIGHT FULL RUDDER!"

And I reached out and pushed a big red button in the middle of the control panel.

"NO! WAIT!" screamed the captain. "DON'T PUSH THAT B—"

But it was too late. Because suddenly the captain was upside down. We were *all* upside down! And spinning!

"ALL AHEAD FULL!" I shouted. I pressed five or six more buttons.

The spaceship began to do loops...
and nosedives...
and spinouts...
and cartwheels...
Luckily, Billy and I had good, firm grips. Billy held on to me, and I held on to the captain. But the captain was the weak link. He forgot to hold on to anything.

So the three of us bounced and rolled and flew from one end of the spaceship to the other. Up and down hallways. Into the engine room. Through the mess hall. Into nooks and out of crannies.

The crew did a lot of traveling, too. Once we passed the two-headed guy as we were rolling out of the engine room. He was on his way in, sliding along at about sixty miles an hour. There were

looks of terror on both of his faces.

A little later, the yellow fellow with the busy feet sailed by. "AAAAAAAA!!!" he said.

Suddenly, the wild spinning stopped. Everything was quiet.

I don't know what happened. Maybe the little yellow fellow kicked the right button as he flew by. All I know is that the roller coaster ride was over.

6

Billy and I climbed off the captain. We helped him to his feet.

"Is it always this bumpy?" I asked politely.

"Earthling!" yelled Captain Thorst. "You...you..."

He tried to say more, but he was too upset to talk.

Finally he staggered over to the control panel, shaking his head and muttering to himself.

As we followed him, Billy nudged me with his elbow and grinned.

"Keep it up, Tod," he whispered.

"You're doing great."

Captain Thorst held on to the control panel to steady himself. He was still a little dizzy. After a minute he took off his jacket, rolled up his sleeves, and shouted an order to his crew. Then he reached for a black knob.

"More loops?" Billy asked eagerly.

"No loops!" boomed the captain. "I'm just turning off the engines. I have to check our forward thrusters. They're probably a mess, after what *he* did."

He glared at me.

"We're going to stop?" I asked. "Then let us give you a hand."

Billy and I ran to a porthole. All we could see was the black emptiness of space. As the engines slowed to a stop, I called to the captain. "Easy does it, Captain. Slower....A little to the

36

left.... A little more.... *Stop*."

"Perfect spot," Billy called. "Doesn't seem to be much traffic around."

Captain Thorst beat his head one, two, three times against a computer.

"Traffic!" he yelled. "There isn't any traffic for two million miles in any direction!"

He grumbled and snorted as he began to test the forward thrusters.

Just then I noticed the microphone for the spaceship intercom lying on a table. I picked it up. I had always wanted to talk to a whole spaceship.

"Attention! Attention!" I shouted into the mike. *"May I have your attention, please!* This is Tod Davis speaking. As you know, we have just had an emergency here in the spaceship. Fortunately, the danger is over. I want

to congratulate you all for a job well done. Every creature did his duty. Oh, and one more thing. Could you guys down in the kitchen send me up a bacon, lettuce, and tomato sandwich? On whole wheat br—"

The captain yanked the mike away.

"Enough!" he yelled. He held his head with both hands and turned to the two-headed alien. "Take charge while I'm gone," he said. "I'm going down to sick bay to see the doctor. These Earthlings have given me a headache."

He gave Billy and me a hard look.

"I'll deal with you two when I get back," he said.

And he stomped out of the control room.

7

"Hike!" I cried.

A huge blue-and-green creature hiked me the football between his legs.

It had been ten minutes since the captain went down to sick bay, and he still hadn't come back. But Billy and I hadn't wasted any time. We taught the crew how to play touch football.

As soon as we explained the rules, all the creatures wanted to play. They liked the idea of football a lot. Especially the blocking. A lot of them were pretty big, and they couldn't wait to try.

Right away we divided up into two

teams. I was captain of one team, and the two-headed guy was captain of the other.

The hard part was finding a football. No one on the spaceship had any kind of ball. But luckily, Captain Thorst had left his jacket on the back of his chair. We decided to use it. We wadded it up, wrapped its arms around it, and tied it up tight. It was a little lopsided, but it made a pretty good football.

At the moment the score was still zero to zero. But the game was heating up fast.

As soon as the blue-and-green creature hiked the ball to me, all the other creatures went into action. Everywhere they were rushing, diving, blocking, tripping, and leaping. The air was filled with yelling,

growling, and howling.

I caught the ball and ran to the left. Than I cut back to the right.

An enormous furry thing with a lot of arms was thundering toward me. The purple creature with all the teeth blocked him hard with his shoulder. "Oof!" said the furry thing as he fell over backward.

I handed the ball off to Billy. Billy faded back to pass.

I felt something at my feet, and I looked down. It was the little yellow fellow. He was busily kicking my foot. He was on my team, but I can't say that he was helping much.

Billy was about to pass the ball. A creature with a long snout and webbed feet tried to tackle him, but Billy leaped out of the way. The creature belly-flopped onto the floor and slid into a computer.

"NO TACKLING!" I shouted. "THIS IS *TOUCH* FOOTBALL!"

Billy passed the ball. But he was off balance. The pass went wild.

With a whoop of glee, the two-headed guy leaped into the air and intercepted the ball. He tucked it under his arm and charged our way. He could really move on those three legs.

Nothing could stop him.

He leaped over a snakelike creature who was trying to trip him. He stiff-armed a tall, green, bug-eyed thing out of his way. He galloped across the goal line.

He'd made a touchdown!

His team began cheering and snorting and grunting with joy. The walls of the control room shook.

The door opened. Captain Thorst walked in.

He took one look around the control room and stopped short.

His mouth dropped open.

"WHAT'S GOING ON HERE?" he roared.

Instantly there was silence. All eyes turned toward the captain.

"Uh-oh," said someone.

There was a burst of activity as the crew scrambled, dived, or tiptoed back to their work stations. Then they tried to look very busy. They were still huffing and puffing, but they tried to look normal.

The two-headed guy hurried over to the captain. Billy and I did, too.

"Well?" demanded Captain Thorst,

glaring at the three of us. "What's going on here?"

"We were playing touch football," I said cheerfully.

"I'm captain of the Kanthor Wild-cats," said the two-headed guy.

Captain Thorst stared at him.

"You're *what*?"

"I'm captain of the Kanthor Wildcats."

Captain Thorst stared at him some more. His eyes were bulging. He looked pretty upset.

Suddenly he caught sight of the football. It was still tucked under the two-headed guy's arm, but it was coming untied.

Captain Thorst pointed at it. "What's that?" he demanded.

"The football, sir," said the two-headed guy.

The captain leaned forward and peered at it closely. His orange skin began to turn red. He looked like he was about to pop.

"You're using my jacket as a foot-ball?" he burst out.

"I scored a touchdown with it, sir," said the two-headed guy proudly.

The captain sputtered. His mouth was moving but he couldn't seem to speak.

I cleared my throat.

"If I may say something, sir," I said. "Your crew has a lot of talent. I think Billy and I can whip them into a top-notch football team. It'll take time, of course. But then we've got lots of time."

Captain Thorst made a choking sound. By now he was bright red.

"That does it!" he exploded. He turned to the two-headed alien. "Turn this ship around!" he said. "We're taking these troublemakers back to Earth!"

8

Billy and I tried to look disappointed about going home.

"But Captain," I said, "we can't leave now. We haven't even taught your crew to play soccer yet."

"Yeah," said Billy. "We could play soccer using the whole spaceship."

"Soccer, my foot!" said the captain. "You two are going home, or my name isn't Captain Zerkfield Thorst!"

The spaceship made a sharp turn. Twenty minutes later the Earth came back into view.

As we slipped into the atmosphere

and headed for home, Billy and I said good-bye to the captain.

"So long, Captain," I said.

"Thanks for the ride," said Billy.

"What's soccer?" asked the two-headed alien.

"Never mind!" said the captain.

A few minutes later we were ready to beam down. Just before we left, I looked down and saw the little yellow fellow. I gave him a big good-bye. He was very nice about it. He gave me a big kick.

Then, suddenly—*ZAP! WHOOSH!*—Billy and I were standing in the middle of the soccer field in Grant Park. The spaceship was disappearing like a silver streak into the clear blue sky.

"We did it!" we cried together. We leaped and shouted and whacked each other on the back.

"I have to hand it to you, Tod," said Billy. "You really were more trouble than you're worth."

"Gee, thanks, Billy," I said, grinning. "You were more trouble than you're worth, too!"

Billy grinned. "It was nothing," he said.

He glanced at his watch. "It's after twelve!" he said. "Now we're *really* going to be late for lunch."

We started toward Billy's house on the double.

"Maybe so," I said as we ran. "But at least we're not going to be thirty years late!"